Brave
Little Owl

by Penny Little
Illustrated by Sean Julian

RED FOX

For my brothers, Simon and Jonny,
who dared me to climb the tallest trees with them,
and only teased me a bit! – PL

For Francesca, Isabel and Valentina.
Three Brave Little Owls. X – SJ

BRAVE LITTLE OWL
A RED FOX BOOK 978 1 782 95572 6
First published in Great Britain by Red Fox,
an imprint of Random House Children's Publishers UK
A Random House Group Company
This edition published 2012
1 3 5 7 9 10 8 6 4 2
Text copyright © Penny Little, 2012
Illustrations copyright © Sean Julian, 2012
The right of Penny Little and Sean Julian to be identified as the author and illustrator of this
work has been asserted in accordance with the Copyright, Designs and Patents Act 1988.
Red Fox Books are published by Random House Children's Publishers UK
61–63 Uxbridge Road, London W5 5SA
www.randomhouse.co.uk
Addresses for companies within The Random House Group Limited can be found at:
www.randomhouse.co.uk/offices.htm
THE RANDOM HOUSE GROUP Limited Reg. No. 954009
A CIP catalogue record for this book is available from the British Library.
Printed in China

Mummy and Daddy Owl were out hunting and
Grandpa Owl was babysitting. 'Go to sleep, all of you,
and no messing around,' he whispered. 'It's Grandma Owl's
birthday tomorrow and I've got to think of a really
special present for her.'

'Oh, let us help, Grandpa, please, pleeease!' begged the biggest baby. 'We've got lots of good ideas!'
'Oh, all right,' sighed Grandpa Owl. 'So what do *you* think would be her best present ever?'

'For you to teach us to fly!' shouted the twins.
'We're really not sleepy at all and we're big enough.'
'Now that *is* a good idea!' grinned Grandpa Owl.
'But where's Little Owl?'

'I'm asleep,' said a tiny voice.
'You can't talk if you're asleep!' teased the boys.
'You're just a scaredy owl!'

'NO, I AM NOT!' shouted Little Owl.

But she shivered a bit as she peeped out of the nest.
The ground seemed a very long way down.

'Come on, all of you,' said Grandpa Owl.
'Line up in a row and copy me.'

'We're going first!' shouted the twins,
elbowing past their big brother.

'No, I'm the oldest so I go first,' said the biggest baby, making the branch sway scarily. 'Move over or I'll push you off.'

'That's enough squabbling,' said Grandpa Owl firmly.
'Now be careful or–'

Splosh!

Little Owl had
slipped and fallen
off the branch.

'Little Owl can't fly . . . but she can swim!'
hooted the boys. Grandpa Owl gave them a fierce
glare, then swooped down to scoop her up.

Back on the branch Little Owl fluffed up her feathers
crossly, spraying her brothers with muddy water.
'Yuck! Stop!' they squealed.

'Now, let's try again,' sighed Grandpa Owl.
'Open your wings, lean forward and–'

Oops!

Little Owl slipped again and dangled upside down from
the branch! 'Stop laughing, you lot,' said Grandpa Owl sternly.
'Not everyone is good at everything – it takes practice.'

'Now, let's see if we can all fly to that old tree on the other side of the woods,' he said.

'Ready. . . steady. . . go!'

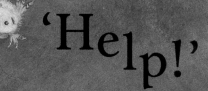

'Help!'

cried Little Owl as she
tumbled from the branch.

Little Owl fell and landed with a . . .

Crash!

'Oooooof!' gasped Baby Badger.
'I thought owls could fly!'

'They can,' sniffed Little Owl sadly. 'Every owl except me,' and big fat tears rolled down her feathery cheeks and plopped on to the ground. 'My brothers were right – I am a scaredy owl.'

'Lots of things can seem scary until you try them,'
said Baby Badger gently. 'I used to be scared of
my dark burrow, but now it's not scary at all.'

'And I was scared of heights,' said Little Squirrel scampering
down the nearest tree. 'But just look at me now!'

But Little Owl felt too sad to try again.
It was growing cold and she couldn't even
get back to her cosy nest.

Suddenly a dark shadow passed over the moon . . .

As Grandpa watched, Little Owl started to run.
She felt the breeze tug at her as it lifted her gently off the hillside.
To her surprise, her wings seemed to know exactly what to do on their own.
Flapping and gliding, she rose higher and higher into the starry night.
'Look at me!' she hooted happily to her friends.

Grandpa Owl flew up to join Little Owl, and together they flew over the meadow to the other side of the wood, where Grandma Owl and all the other grandchildren were waiting for them.

Everyone cheered as Little Owl landed.
'You're the best birthday present ever!' whispered Grandma Owl.
'And you are a very brave little owl.'

Little Owl never forgot the special night she learned to fly and, as she grew bigger and stronger, she always loved to soar through the sky under the beautiful bright silver moon.